DOWNTOWN

DOWNTOWN

Ginger Henry Kuenzel

Published by Different Viewpoint Publishing

Copyright © 2019 by Different Viewpoint
Ginger Henry Kuenzel

ISBN: 9781796531886

Table of Contents

*This book is dedicated to the people
who live in small towns across America*

Downtown is a tribute to the people in small towns across America who are the threads and the dye in the fabric of our society – holding it together and giving it color. They are the ones who run the small businesses, volunteer as emergency services personnel, organize 4th of July parades, drive neighbors to doctors' appointments and raise funds to help the less fortunate. In working together to better their communities, the people of America's small towns don't let their political differences divide them. They work shoulder-to-shoulder with their neighbors, they find solutions, and, when necessary, they seek compromises. They are role models, showing us how we can join together to achieve a common goal, despite our differences. It is they who can lead the way in setting a new course for our country – a course toward a more caring, more humane, more united society. A course toward a future in which we are proud of all that is good about America and are working together to find viable solutions to our problems. This is who we are.

Preface

Sitting at our regular highboy table in the back corner of The Pour Choices Bar & Grille every Thursday night, making one pour choice after another, Sally and I delighted in regaling each other with stories about life in our small town. When we first started doing this, the rumor spread quickly that we were writing a book. We did little – well, if truth be known, nothing – to disavow this. And so, friends would stop by our table to make inane comments like, "Just so you know, I'm not going to buy your book until it comes out in paperback."

"Good to know," I said to Sally. "We can use that quote on the jacket of the hardback, along with all the other stellar one-line reviews we're hearing."

Friends frequently asked, "Tell me, am I going to be in your book?" Our standard response – spoken with a not-so-discreet roll of the eyes – was, "Oh, don't worry!" And, of course, those people immediately set about doing just that: worrying. Wait, they wondered, did that mean that they *weren't* going to be in the book? In their eyes, this was clearly a fate worse than actually being in the book. Many of them launched into lengthy discourses, spilling all the things they had done that they felt were indeed worthy of a mention in the book. "We'll think about it," we'd tell them. "We have to see if we have enough pages."

The result was that we simply couldn't make any headway with our stories, what with all these characters installing themselves at our table and pleading their case.

"Can't you just make them go away?" I asked Sally one evening after listening to one particularly chatty friend for far too long.

"No," she replied. "I think it's more likely that they're going to make *us* go away."

Suddenly it hit me. That's what I would do – set off on a road trip of indeterminate length. The point would simply be to encounter and observe people in other small towns across America. I'd have to go by myself since Sally had far too many commitments and needed to stay in town. It's better to go on a trip like this alone anyway, I told myself. It will force me to talk to strangers instead of a sidekick. And so that's just what I did.

The point is that the characters in this book are not real. They are a composite of people who live in small towns all across America. It's entirely fiction, people. So, if you think you recognize yourself or someone you know in one of the chapters, my advice to you is: Get over it! Any similarities to real people are completely a figment of your – and my – imagination. And so, fasten your seatbelt and come with me on a visit to the town of Downtown.

How Downtown got its name

Our town wasn't always called Downtown. It used to be called… Oh, wait. I am not at liberty to divulge that. You see, the thing is that there was another town — well, actually, a city — that had already laid claim to our name. They threatened to sue if we didn't "cease and desist from positioning ourselves as something we weren't." That was the exact language they used in the somewhat ornery letter that they sent to our mayor some years ago, the original of which is safely kept in our town vault.

Our town board members were absolutely certain that our town had acquired its name long, long before that other city. But, since Downtown is so small that it doesn't even appear on most maps, they figured this

1

wasn't a battle that they had any hope of winning. After all, they weren't even sure they could prove that the town existed.

The only recourse was to hold a special meeting to come up with a new name for our town. Ernest, the mayor and self-proclaimed visionary, argued that it should be something unique, a name that people would remember and that no other town would ever want to later claim as their own. "Something that would put us on the map!" he exclaimed. The board members agreed. After all, they certainly didn't want to have to go through this process again. They really hated meetings.

"How about if we do something like that town with the ground hog in Pennsylvania did?" Ernest suggested.

"Ain't nobody in these parts that knows how to pronounce that town's name. And they sure as Hell can't spell it," Frank objected. The other town board members nodded in agreement and quickly nixed the idea.

"No, no, no," Ernest said. "You don't get it. We're not gonna use their name. That'd put us right back where we started. What I'm thinking is that that town has gained fame and fortune by using that silly little groundhog and its shadow," he explained. "We have geese everywhere here. And I say we use them to make us famous. And it could also give us the perfect name for our town."

"Gooseville?" George scoffed.

"No," Ernest said. "You know how everyone in town hates those geese. They crap in our lake, make a mess on our lawns, not to mention the town park. Billy absolutely refuses to mow there ever since his tractor blade hit that really big pile of... well, you know, and he got what he called a facial treatment." The board members all laughed, remembering how Betty, the town clerk, described what Billy looked like when he stormed into the town hall with the tractor keys that day. "Need I say more?" Ernest continued. "I've been thinkin' about this and I have some ideas about how we can kill two birds with one stone. So to speak."

He launched into an explanation of how the town could attract businesses that produce down products – using the geese, of course. He was certain that this would create an economic boom in the town. Once companies saw all the geese that the town had to offer, they would be eager to build factories and start producing down comforters, down jackets, down vests, down mittens, down pillows and more. The possibilities could be endless, he added. The others on the town board, listening attentively as Ernest laid out his plan, nodded and agreed that they couldn't find any 'down' side to this idea. And, said Ernest excitedly, this would also solve their dilemma about a name for the town. They would rename it Downtown.

The excitement among the town board members was becoming evident. George proposed that someone might be able to open a cooking school. "I even got a name for it," he said with a chuckle. "What do you think about 'Your Goose is Cooked?'"

"Great idea!" Frank said. "And Betty can get her Senior Club to put together a cookbook of goose recipes and sell it to get money for all those trips they take."

Of course, all of the goose meat would be organic, free-range, raised on the world's cleanest water, Ernest pointed out. And, since Downtown is situated on the shores of a spring-fed lake, the meat could clearly be marketed as spring-fed. Rick chimed in that he thought they should also feed the geese in the other seasons as well. "You know, we don't want the geese dying on us," he said.

Charlie had remained quiet, which was very unlike him. He was lost in his own thoughts about how he might start bottling vodka as a side business. He would use the town's spring-fed lake water, put pictures of the geese on the label and call it Fifty Shades Goose Vodka. The definition of distilling, he reasoned to himself, is that you take a large quantity of something and make it more concentrated. Well, there was a very large quantity of geese. And of water. He remembered hearing somewhere that Russians will travel to any place that serves vodka, so he figured he could attract foreign tourists to Downtown with his new product. This would further contribute to the town's economic development and position it as an international tourist destination. He also thought he might be able to repurpose some of the equipment from the abandoned mines in the hills above town and build a still up there. It would be out of sight -- just in case some pesky members of law enforcement started snooping around. And, he figured, if need be, he could just hide everything in the mines until the danger had passed. It probably wouldn't be a problem anyway since Downtown isn't exactly on the sheriff's radar, let alone any regular patrol route.

"What are you smiling about?" George asked Charlie, jarring him back to the present.

"Oh, nothin'," Charlie said. "I was just thinkin' that if we can't agree on the name Downtown, I might have another idea."

"What's that?" asked Ernest.

"Well, I was kinda thinkin' that I like the sound of the name Stillwater," Charlie answered.

"Nope," George said. "I've heard that name before." He explained that he had read an article in the paper not too long ago that made him laugh so hard that the town's name had stuck in his mind: Stillwater. It seems that a town employee there got himself arrested for falsifying his urine during a drug test. "He ordered a fake... well, how should I call it, manly body part online to trick the testers into thinking it was his pee going into the cup," George said. "I still don't know how he did it, but it made me laugh so hard that I almost peed in my own pants." No, Stillwater wasn't a name they could even consider.

As the special meeting drew to a close, it was clear that the town board members were exceptionally pleased with themselves. In the course of just one relatively short special session, they had come up with not only a new name for the town but also an expansive and comprehensive plan for the town's future development. "People around here can be damned glad that they've got us in charge," George said to Ernest as they walked out of the building.

"Yup, that's why they keep electing us," Ernest said.

That and the fact that nobody else ever runs, he thought to himself.

Between a rock
and a hard spot

The people who sit on the Downtown planning, zoning and town boards are volunteers, and thus not always top experts in the matters at hand. And, although it wouldn't really be fair to say that they play favorites – based on factors like how long you've lived in the town, whether or not your sister is married to their son's wife's nephew, or whether they like the cookies you baked for the meeting – there definitely seems to be little rhyme or reason to why these boards approve some building projects without batting an eye while giving a thumbs down to others.

For instance, there was Joe – who ran into problems with the zoning board when he placed a wooden gazebo on his lawn near the lake. He had been enjoying his new gazebo for some time when suddenly the zoning board decided that he was not allowed to have a structure so close to the shoreline. "This here thing, whatever you call it, has gotta be set back 75 feet from the lake," the zoning administrator told him in no uncertain terms. Since there was no room for the gazebo anywhere else on the property, Joe decided he would need to get creative. "My dream was to have a gazebo on the lake," he recalls. "So I decided I would simply have to take that literally."

Joe called the Department of Motor Vehicles to find out what the requirements were for building a boat. He learned that he would merely need to fill out a form, have the vessel inspected once it was built and be assigned an identification number. He set about constructing a pontoon-style boat, added an outboard motor and running lights, and placed his gazebo atop it. And since there's no law that says you can't have a boat on your property, he situated it on his front lawn, even closer to the lake than where the gazebo originally had been. So now Joe is back in his gazebo once again enjoying his expansive view of the lake and listening to the gentle lapping of the waves on the shore. The town, whose original intent was to have the gazebo moved further back from the lake, must now live with the fact that it's even closer to the water's edge. What's more, Joe has the added advantage of being able to launch his gazebo and cruise down the lake whenever he gets tired of the view from his own lawn.

There was also the time that Mildred came to a town board meeting to ask if she could have a tree planted in the town park to honor her husband, a former town board member who had passed away. They approved her request and even said that the town would order a plaque with her husband's name to mount on a stone beside the tree.

In the following years, Mildred frequently sat under the tree, enjoying the serenity of the town park. But one day, when she arrived in the park, she noticed a hole where the stone with the plaque had been. She drove immediately to the town offices to find out what had happened. Ernest, the mayor, explained that the town had to have it removed because a visitor to the park had complained that the rock was a hazard.

"A hazard?" Mildred asked. "How's that?"

"Well, the visitor said he was concerned that someone could trip over it, fall down and then sue the town," Ernest said.

"That's completely ridiculous," Mildred exclaimed. "The rock was right next to the tree. If a person can't see the rock or the tree, they shouldn't be walking around in the park. And by the way, the lake is right there, too, so they might fall in and drown. I reckon that would also be cause for a lawsuit against the town."

"Calm down, Mildred," Ernest said. "Some people also thought that the rock was unsightly. So we moved it over to that pile of rocks at the north side of the park. It won't bother anyone there."

"Bother anyone? That's not the point," Mildred protested. "The rock with the plaque is supposed to be next to the tree, to honor Calvin's memory."

Ernest, who detested any kind of confrontation, told Mildred that she should come to the next town board to plead her case. At that meeting, a lengthy discussion ensued among the board members. George argued, "Our park is becoming littered with trees and rocks. We have to put an end to it." Mildred countered that she had been in many parks around the country during her lifetime and had noticed that trees and rocks were an integral part of every single park she'd visited. Finally, Charlie abruptly ended the discussion by offering a resolution stating that there could be no new trees, rocks or plaques placed in the park ever again. This was immediately seconded and approved, after which an audience member stood up and asked, "What if a tree dies and needs to be replaced?" This was rather embarrassing to the board since they hadn't thought of this eventuality. Their solution was to simply move on to other business. Case closed!

As the meeting drew to an end an hour later, George mentioned that a service organization in town wanted to make a donation to purchase a new lifeguard chair for the park. The board agreed that this was a nice gesture, and they voted to accept the money. The only thing that the organization wanted in return, George said, was a plaque on the chair stating that it was a gift from them.

All board members agreed that this was reasonable, at which point Mildred stood up and reminded them that, according to the resolution they had passed just an hour earlier, new plaques in the park are now banned. The town clerk nodded and held up the paper with her meeting minutes. "Mildred's right," she said. The town board had placed themselves firmly between a rock and a hard spot. Their solution? Adjourn the meeting and think about it next month.

Running for town board

Karen decided several years ago that she wanted to get a seat at the table – the town board table. The only way for her to do this was to win an election. When she mentioned to us what she was thinking, we said, pretty much in unison: "Run, run, run!" She took that as encouragement. It was only later that it occurred to her that what we really meant was, "Are you crazy? Run, don't walk, away from this ridiculous notion." By the way, isn't it weird that, in Great Britain, people stand for election, but here in the U.S., we run?

Once we realized that there was no talking Karen out of her crazy notion about running – toward the office, not away – we all agreed to help with her campaign. We obtained from the Board of Elections a list of all the registered voters in town and went through it name by name. With only 534 people on the list, it turned out that, among us, we knew just about every one of them. It took several meetings to actually get through the list. After all, there were a lot of stories to be told about the individual voters. And we were interested in hearing every single one of them. Suzanne, for instance, gave us the lowdown on who was spending the night with whom last winter. How did she know? It seems that her brother was driving the town snow plow, which meant that he was out clearing the roads in the early morning hours and saw exactly whose pick-up truck was parked at whose house.

But it wasn't just at the campaign committee meetings that we heard stories. We accompanied Karen as she knocked on doors, talking to voters personally, listening to their concerns and telling them how she could help them. But we also had some concerns. One of these was the fact that everyone in town seems to have ferocious dogs. It's a good thing that none of us are scared of dogs or our political aspirations for Karen might have ended early in the game. We also learned that it's best not to get too deep into conversations, particularly about non-political issues. There was Mark, for instance, who told us how lonely he has been since his wife died five years ago. His daughter recently took him to a Senior Club meeting in the next town, he said, but he didn't enjoy that at all: "I was the only man there and the women were all old." Yeah, isn't that generally how it is at a

Seniors Club? Mark also told us about his forays into online dating and how unsuccessful that had been. It's a fine line when campaigning – you want to listen to people's issues, but there are some things you just can't help with!In the end, when all the votes were counted, it was apparent that Karen wouldn't be helping anyone with anything. The townspeople decided to stick with the good old town board members that they already knew and loved.

Winter in Downtown

Downtown is pretty dead in the winter. At least that's what the tourists and those who own vacation homes think. After all, they come to swim, boat, sit on their dock and make small talk at cocktail parties. They can't imagine anything worse than sticking around for the desolate days of winter, when snowfalls are measured in feet and temperatures can sometimes hover around zero for days at a time. The only restaurant in town closes down in September and doesn't reopen until June. And even the general store closes for several months during the cold months. "Why on earth would you want to stay here in winter?" It's the question we hear again and again from friends who pack up each September and return in June. We smile and nod, tell them to have a great winter and that we'll see them next summer. We wave as they drive out of town. And we breathe a sigh of relief.

Don't get me wrong – we all love the summer months, too. And we love our summer friends. But we also love it when they leave, and we take the town back for ourselves.

The 'year-rounders' are a special breed. We rely on each other for entertainment. It's always easy to find at least a couple of friends who are up for snowshoeing, cross-country skiing or hiking, depending on the weather and the snow pack. And if it's nasty outside, we might get together for board games. Or a potluck dinner.

Perhaps best of all is our regular Wednesday 'Craft Night.' Sometimes we have food, sometimes not. But we always have libations. Laurie, who originated the concept a few years ago, says it really should be called 'task night.' Her idea was for everyone to bring a project that she had been meaning to get to, but just could never find the time. That might consist of putting photos in an album, deleting emails from an overfilled inbox, wrapping Christmas presents, sewing buttons on a shirt – or perhaps even a real craft, like making birch bark picture frames. We could get our tasks completed while enjoying drinks and good conversation.

Over time, the definition of 'craft' has gotten looser and looser: On any given night, Teresa might be helping Suzanne color her hair, Sharon could be painting a bird house or Tammy might be writing a new profile for her match.com page. We're pretty tolerant when it comes to defining the term 'craft.' We did at one point, however, have to lay down the law and ban the removal of body parts when Bonnie decided that craft night would be a good time to clip her toenails. But always, we are perfecting the fine craft of drinking wine – though not necessarily the craft of drinking fine wine. Husbands, wusbands and boyfriends are generally not involved – they prefer to watch a ball game or play pool.

One fall, late into the evening and far into the wine bottles, we got to talking about how horrible March is in Downtown. It's when mud season sets in and just getting out of your driveway can require an all-terrain vehicle, chains, cranes and lifts. The snow is gone – or too mushy to be enjoyable – and everyone is anxious for winter to be over. We started thinking that we should go somewhere to escape. Somewhere like Paris, someone said. Since many of our Craft Night conversations tend to involve life-changing ideas like winning the lottery, writing a best-selling novel or convincing George Clooney to stop by during one of our Craft Nights, the idea of a trip to Paris fit right into the concept: nice to think about, but probably not gonna happen. Nevertheless, we started checking out airfares, and before we knew it, we had found a great price and were booking our tickets.

To make a long story short, we didn't spend mud season in Downtown that year. Of course, not everyone in the group went on the trip. Some thought that Clooney might pick the week that we were gone to show up at Craft Night. Or that it might be the week that someone had a winning lottery ticket. But the rest of us figured that if we could create so much fun here in Downtown, where there is absolutely nothing going on in the early spring, then think about the excitement that would lie in store for us in Paris! Certainly nobody can say about us that we're stick-in-the-muds. That term will be reserved for those who stayed behind. I'm pretty sure that they didn't enjoy mud season that year any more than all the other years!

Property management for snowbirds

Each year, around May, all those summer folks who can't fathom life in Downtown in the winter start planning their return. To make things easier for them, I thought it would be a good idea to let them know ahead of time what they should expect when they come back. So, I spoke with our local newspaper editor, and she agreed to publish a short article about what had been going on in Downtown during the long winter months, just so there would be no surprises.

Those of us who stay in Downtown all year – after all, someone has to be here to roll up the sidewalks each fall – are anxiously anticipating your return. To be honest, we've grown a bit tired of hanging out with the same 13 people all winter. We need more people! But we manage.

If you wonder what the heck we do in Downtown all winter, let me explain. First of all, it takes us about a month to get all those sidewalks rolled up and stored. After that, since nothing in town is open, we start partying at each others' homes. But by January, that gets pretty old, and we're tired of the same old haunts all the time. That's when we start thinking about where else we could go. So many of you have such beautiful homes, and we are certain that you are happy to have us drop by occasionally. After all, it's mutually beneficial. It helps us deal with our horrific cases of cabin fever, and it helps you by giving your place that 'lived in' look. You know, lots of cars in the driveway, lights on all over the house, music blaring.

And now, since we know that many of you will be heading back to Downtown very shortly for the summer season, we thought it would be a good idea to update you on some things you might want to know in terms of your house here and what you might want to consider bringing with you.

Janet and Brian – We discovered that you moved your key to a new hiding place before you left last fall. You rascals! To be honest, it was a bit of a nuisance when we arrived at your place for our party and the key wasn't in its normal spot. We were highly motivated to find it, since the mercury was hovering at around 10 below and we needed to get inside. We did locate it pretty quickly, so no worries. In fact, it seemed a bit too easy, and we worried – on your behalf, of course – that burglars or other undesirables might also have no trouble finding it.

So we decided that it would be best to hide it in a far safer place. Good luck finding it!

Susie and Peter – The liquor at your place was really not the best. In fact, we even thought we might have to go out and get some replacements. But the roads were icy and there aren't any liquor stores anywhere close, as you know, so we had to settle for your bottom-shelf stuff. But come on, do you really serve that rock-gut to your guests? We suggest that you stop on the way up here and get some better quality booze. You'll need a new supply anyway since we managed to polish it all off. It wasn't easy, but somebody had to do it, and we knew that you'd thank us.

Beth and Scott – Did you know that the flue in your fireplace has some issues? Either that or we just couldn't figure it out. Anyway, the house got kind of smoky when we lit the fire. It sure didn't make for a fun evening, but no worries. It's just that the walls got really sooty. We felt bad, so we painted them all black and so you probably won't even notice the soot. Of course, if you don't like the idea of black walls, you might want to bring up a few cans of another color of paint when you come.

Suzanne and Jack – With all your plants, we found your home to be like a tropical oasis in the frozen tundra of Downtown. We knew you'd appreciate us coming by frequently to water, and while there, we of course made ourselves at home. We knew you'd also want us to do that. And then, one evening, someone opened a drawer to get a corkscrew and it was completely filled with water. Also, because we of course always take off our shoes (we're that kind of guests), we noticed that our socks were getting really wet from walking around on your carpet. That's when we realized that your plants are all fake and our watering was for naught. Now the problem is that your carpeting has taken on a kind of musty smell. You'll be glad to know that we're not partying there anymore since we can't take the odor. By the way, you might want to bring up a bunch of towels when you come. And probably also some new carpet samples.

If any others of you are worried about what might have been going on in your house over the winter, we'll be happy to stop by and check things out for you. And yes, we've already gotten the sidewalks out of storage and rolled them out again. So, everything is all ready for your return!

It's a strange thing – ever since I sent out that email, more and more people who used to not want to be caught dead in Downtown in the winter are now starting to make more and more frequent appearances during the off-season months. Heck, we might even have to stop putting away the sidewalks for the winter.

Houseguests

When I was growing up, my parents were happy to welcome guests for a short stay. But they were just as happy to see them go. And, just in case any guests might think about settling in for a longer stay, the sign hanging in our guestroom was enough to make them reconsider. It read: "Guests, like fish, tend to stink after three days." My parents didn't believe in beating around the bush.

There are a few certainties in life: Death. Taxes. Sunrise. Sunset. And – when you live in Downtown, on the shores of a beautiful mountain lake – houseguests. Yes, indeed. Friends and relatives are certain to descend on you every summer. They don't come in April when the plague of cabin fever lies over the town and you'd give your eye tooth for some company. Or in November, when the days are dreary. No, they of course come in summer. During July and August, it's all I can do to keep my calendar updated and the sheets and towels washed and ready for the next onslaught.

Over the years, I've experienced many different types of guests. There are those who are truly a delight to have around. And there are those who are – quite frankly – not. My favorite guests are the ones who make themselves at home. When they're thirsty, they go to the fridge and get themselves something to drink. In the morning, they don't wait around for me to wake up, but instead head straight to the kitchen and start the coffee brewing. If we're running low on milk, they go to the store and pick some up. They don't constantly ask what they can do to help. They simply do it. In short, they make my life easy! On the other end of the spectrum are those who need to be waited on hand and foot. They take great care to tell me – over and over again – that they don't want me to go out of the way on their behalf. And then they stand around and wait for me to do exactly that.

Another pet peeve are the guests who bring along – yes, you guessed it – their pets. It's not that I have anything against animals, as long as they're well behaved and the owner clearly understands that they need to be kept in their place. In other words, Fido does *not* need to sit on the sofa to watch TV with us and he also doesn't need to sleep in their bed or eat his dinner at our table. And does Rover really have to bark ferociously and jump up on me to lick my face every time I enter the house? I'm glad to know that he's keeping strangers at bay – but hey, remember, I'm not the one who's a stranger here.

And then there are those guests who think it's perfectly okay to bring along extra people. Some are convinced that their child needs to have a friend along to play with. I once had a couple visiting from Europe who informed me that they wanted to meet up with a distant cousin who had moved to the United States years ago. "Great idea!" I said, happy to hear that they would finally be moving on to their next destination. However, as it turned out, 'meeting up' with this cousin meant inviting him to my house for a visit. After all, they were absolutely certain that he'd enjoy my house and beach just as much as they did.

This past summer, my friend Keith came to visit. He recently has become a passionate advocate for energy-efficient lighting and thus brought along a stash of energy-saving bulbs. He wanted to help me see the light about how much better off I would be with them. I didn't really mind. However, when we were invited to my friend Valerie's house for dinner and he disappeared during the meal, I started to worry. As we were discussing where Keith could possibly be, the room suddenly went dark. It turned out that he had gone to the basement to replace some of Valerie's bulbs. But because it was an older house with outdated electrical circuits, he had blown a fuse. Perhaps he was simply proving that there's more than one way to save electricity.

Some houseguests simply don't pass the "Lake Test." They head for the shower every time they come into the house after a swim in the lake – which is so clean that people drink it. And they put their bathing suit in the washing machine after every swim. They insist on drinking bottled water, afraid that my well water will give them some sort of incurable disease. I can deal with all that, albeit unwillingly. But here's the real deal breaker: Any guest who doesn't consider a roadtrip to the Downtown dump to be the highlight of their vacation is probably not going to be invited back. After all, it's the social event of the day. But more on that in another chapter.

Of course, family is exempt from any 'houseguest rules.' When my grandchildren arrived for a visit last summer, my granddaughter announced right off the bat that she wanted to try being a vegetarian. The problem is she hates all vegetables. Mealtimes were a challenge during that stay. At least for the first day or two. When her dad brought home steaks for the grill, she decided that she could give up being a vegetarian, at least for that evening. Shortly after they all left, I discovered several untouched containers of tofu in the fridge. Also in the fridge was a carboard container that looked like it came from a Chinese restaurant. But that was a wrong assumption. When I opened it, I saw dirt. With worms crawling through it. Ah, yes, I remembered. The leftovers from my grandson's fishing adventure. But summer is just beginning. Perhaps I can interest my next houseguests in a tofu-centric dinner. I'll refrain from looking for a recipe for the worms. Unless, of course, I decide I don't like those next visitors.

Come winter, when the temps in Downtown fall to the zero point and my beach is covered with snow, when my heating bill is reaching new highs, that might be the time to head south and visit friends in Florida. I know just how to be the perfect houseguest.

Witness protection

Have I mentioned that winters are long and desolate in these parts? The Pour Choices Bar and Grill – the only bar in town – closes from September to May, which is when the tourists start returning. Even the Downtown General Store shuts down for several months. We have no bowling alley, no gas station, no library, no stores. We who stay in Downtown when all those others leave are thus completely on our own at this time of year when it comes to entertainment. Fortunately, that's not a problem. We love to get together and recount tales on long winter nights. Call it revisionist history, or call it simply making things up. Either way, it comes out about the same.

Recently, some of us were talking about which characters in town might be part of the witness protection program. After all, what better place to send people for a life of anonymity? We have a huge influx of people each year when the weather turns warm, and nobody ever asks or cares where they came from. Let's say you've testified against some powerful crime family and need to go into hiding. Downtown is the perfect place for you.

Take the Cranston clan. This extended family arrived from out of nowhere in an RV and parked it behind an abandoned restaurant. This eatery was no longer in business because it had been taken over by the federal government after the owners were caught selling illegal drugs out back. It seems that all those bags of 'flour' in the kitchen weren't actually being used to make pizza. Next thing we knew, the restaurant had an "Open" sign posted and the Cranston family was running the show. Clearly, however, they had absolutely no idea about how to cook, wait on tables or tend bar. In fact, they had not a single skill associated with running a restaurant. The food was generally some kind of mysterious concoction, the drinks were watered down and the service was so slow that guests forgot what they had ordered by the time the food arrived. This was a good thing since the waitresses, the Cranston daughters, also forgot what guests had ordered by the time they got to the kitchen to place the order. One day – or actually one night – the family took off in their RV, never to be seen again.

Tony, another guy who was obviously either from the witness protection program or just a plain criminal trying to go underground, appeared in town about 15 years ago. In the blink of an eye, he became the owner of the local Bed & Breakfast. He hung lots of paintings throughout the house and put an "Art Gallery" sign out front. The gallery was never actually open, and we are fairly certain that it was merely a front. Tony, however, occasionally allow guests to stay overnight. They got a bed, but no breakfast. Tony wasn't an early riser.

There are a few other characters in town who we've pegged as questionable. But we don't ask questions. We don't have to. We already know all the answers – as you can tell. I can't vouch for the authenticity. It could be revisionist history. Or we could just be making things up. I'll never tell.

The Downtown Motel

L ast spring, as the days were getting longer and spring was approaching, I found myself daydreaming about a career change. Something like running a motel. The idea was quite appealing. I could picture myself hanging out on the shores of the lake, relaxing with guests who were thrilled to be here on vacation, spending the entire summer doing everything I could to ensure that my guests were having fun. What could be better?

When I mentioned this idea to my friend Sarah, she hopped on board with it right away. She was downright excited, and we started sketching out plans. The motel would only be open in the summer months. After all, tourists are few and far between in these parts in any other season. And anyway, it would be too expensive to heat the rooms in the winter. Yes, this would definitely be a summer motel.

When we visited the Downtown realtor – yes, there is only one – he told us that the Downtown Motel – yes, there is only one – was for sale. He seemed a bit dubious about the seriousness of our plans, but agreed to show us what he termed the 'perfect' motel property. It had five units, each with a private bath. It looked to me like guests would have to leave the bathroom door open while brushing their teeth if they wanted to avoid suffering serious elbow injury. 'Cozy' came to mind as the term we would use in our marketing brochures.

Behind the motel was a lovely lawn with five cottages, a sandy beach and a relatively large swimming area. This was more like it. We could see definite possibilities for these rustic cabins. Aha, 'rustic.' Another term we could use in marketing. This is, by the way, a term open for interpretation: anything from falling-down-and-needs-mega-work to quaint-picturesque-charming. We recognized that it would require considerable time, effort and money to get from the first interpretation to the second.

Returning to Sarah's house, we mixed ourselves a cool adult beverage and continued mapping out our plans. We should name each cottage, Sarah said, and establish a motif that would define the décor. She suggested names like 'Moose Haven' and 'Robin's Nest.' I noted 'Mouse Haven' and 'Bird Nest in the Tub" might be more appropriate. After all, there are laws about truth in advertising, right?

Sarah was undaunted. We could also set up a quaint café, she continued, where we would serve breakfast. "Fine with me," I said. "But nobody is getting served before 11 am! I like to sleep in." At this point, I could see that Sarah was starting to doubt the wisdom of going into business with me. I quickly allayed her fears by volunteering that I would be willing to staff the reception desk until all hours of the night. I was convinced that there would be all sorts of Jack Kerouac and Willy Nelson characters pulling in during the wee hours. They'd of course want to stay up chatting with me about their adventures on the road. I'd pour them some wine and ply them with questions. Many of them could play bit parts in the novel I'm writing – or more accurately, that I intend to write once I've met enough characters. Yes, nighttime is where I could add value. Of course, that would mean that I couldn't possibly be available to cook breakfast after staying up so late. Come to think of it, all the morning tasks would simply have to be Sarah's responsibility. I was sure she wouldn't mind being the chief cook, bottle washer and chambermaid.

Well, as you might have guessed by now, our idea never came to pass. There were too many things we simply couldn't agree on. And, we decided, we really didn't want to work all that hard during the summertime. That is, after all, the best time to get out and enjoy Downtown... and our summer guests!

Hunting season

People around the world are accustomed to the standard four seasons: spring, summer, fall and winter. Here in Downtown, however, we figure why limit ourselves to just those four. After all, if we were to start thinking in October that the winter season has set in for an interminably long period of time – let's say until late April – well, that can be downright depressing. That's why we divide it up – starting with leaf-peeping season. After that comes the holiday season. Then we're prepared to have a month or so of winter season. This is followed by cabin-fever season, maple sugaring season and then mud season… the list goes on. But you get the picture.

In October, when it's leaf-peeping season, I like to get out in the woods as much as possible. Mysterious animal tracks, herds of wild turkeys, amazing Tarzan-like vines seemingly draped in mid-air, the towering canopy of old-growth trees -- these are just a few of the sights to marvel at during this time of year.

Just yesterday, my friend Patty and I decided to hike to a wonderful little pond near the top of a nearby mountain. The trail is through dark woods along a deeply rutted dirt road that is closed to traffic. It was a beautiful crisp day, and I had dressed appropriately – or so I thought – in jeans and fleece and my favorite patchwork quilt jacket. But one thing I had forgotten to reckon with was that other fall season... namely, hunting season.

"Are you crazy?" Patty asked when she saw me. "You're *not* going to wear that, are you?" At first I thought she meant that I looked far too fashionable for a hike in the woods. But no, that wasn't the issue. She reminded me that, even though hunting season hadn't officially opened, there might be people who like to jump the gun – so to speak – and bag a deer in advance. Oh, and I believe that I failed to mention that my jeans were brown, the fleece was beige and my jacket had a hunter green check pattern overall, a large evergreen tree on the front and a huge moose on the back.

Patty exclaimed that I looked like a sitting duck -- or more appropriately, a walking moose. "Nothing like wearing a target on your back!" she exclaimed with obvious amazement at how naive I was. "Not to mention that there's a reason they call that color you have on HUNTER green."

"Oh, right," I said, slinking back inside to look for something with less animal-like colors. I don't own anything that's fluorescent orange (hate that color). And all my lime green outfits were decidedly too summery -- not to mention far too stylish for a stroll in the woods. But obviously the target-practice jacket would have to go back into the closet.

I settled on a vibrant pink fleece jacket and a bright yellow baseball cap. I figured that, unless the hunters were tracking parrots that day, I'd be safe. And since there is a real dearth of parrots in these parts, chances were that any hunters we'd encounter would realize -- even from afar -- that we were not some wild animal that they might want to hunt.

Unlike me, Patty had carefully planned her outfit in advance. It consisted of a wild assortment of colors: a shocking orange silk scarf knotted in a huge bow around her head, a bright lime green fleece vest, flaming red pants and a backpack the color of a swimming pool floor. "Okay," I said to her. "That might be the sensible thing to wear in the woods during hunting season. But if you ever see me leaving my house in that kind of outlandish garb, please, just shoot me."

The Downtown
Post Office

Although I was born in Downtown, I didn't always live there full-time. School, jobs, wanderlust and a variety of other life experiences took me to other towns and even other countries. Several years ago, however, I decided that the time had come to move back to the place of my roots. One of the first decisions that I had to make was about the mail in my life. Notice that the operative word here is 'mail' and not 'male' – I had already made a decision about the latter. So, in terms of U.S. postal delivery, I could either rent a box at the Downtown Post Office or I could put up a mailbox at the end of my driveway. For me, it was a no-brainer. I love going to the post office to pick up my mail. For one thing, it's a great place to catch up on the latest gossip.

Just like at the Downtown Dump, you're bound to run into someone who has a story to tell – either about themselves or someone else! And even if they don't have a story to tell, they're likely as not to simply make one up, just for conversation. I also knew that having to go to the post office every day would force me to get dressed and out of the house. After all, I planned to make my living by being a freelance writer working at home. And anyone with that kind of lifestyle will tell you that there is a distinct danger of finding yourself still in your pajamas from the night before when it's time to get ready for bed. And there might even be some days when you don't remember whether you already put on your pjs for the night or are still in them from the morning. It could become a problem. And I certainly wanted to avoid it.

But most of all, I love going to the post office because of Carleen, our postmaster, who has held this position since the pony express was phased out. She's extremely friendly, but dislikes any transactions that are out of the ordinary – such as having to sell stamps in more than one denomination. On the other hand, we can always count on her to go above and beyond the call of duty. For instance, if she notices that a letter has been dropped in the mailbox without enough postage, she puts the extra stamps on it rather than returning it to the sender. Then she simply lets you know the next time you come in how much you owe her. She once called me on the phone to tell me I had a package waiting that was so large that it probably would not fit in my car. It turns out that it was a plastic rain barrel that I had ordered. Now, I ask you: How many postmasters know what kind of car you drive? And how many care whether or not your car can accommodate your package? Carleen does. She suggested that I might need to borrow someone's pickup truck. But I was in luck. Paul, who happened to be in the post office at the time, overheard the conversation and offered to drop the package off at my house.

And then there was the time that Craig and Susie were going to be out of town for several days and asked Carleen to hold their mail. What they forgot to take into consideration was that the shipment of baby chicks that they had ordered would arrive while they were away. Carleen decided that she had no choice but to take all the chicks home with her over the weekend. Lucky for Carleen, that was the same weekend that a shipment of wine arrived for Darleen and Mike, who were also out of town and which Carleen also decided she should take home with her.

Shortly after I moved back to Downtown, I was picking up my mail one day when Carleen asked, "Do you know what's going on? I feel like everyone is moving away." Since I know almost everyone in town and I hadn't heard that anyone was making plans to leave, I was perplexed. "What makes you think that?" I asked.

"I keep having to put out more change-of-address packets in the lobby," she explained. "They're disappearing like hotcakes."

Truth be told, I knew exactly what was going on. After all, my friends and I were at least partially – if not fully –

to blame. We had discovered shortly before that these packets included discount coupons from local retail establishments, and we had begun helping ourselves to these coupons. It didn't occur to us that this would create a problem for Carleen. Of course, I couldn't let on that I had played a role in creating the problem. But I came up with a solution: I suggested to Carleen that she keep the packets behind the counter and let people ask her for them. That way, I told her, she could strike up a conversation with people to find out where they were moving to and what it might be like there. After all, Carleen was considering going on a well-deserved winter vacation – and, I told her, what better way to learn about other towns around the country that might be vacation-worthy.

Of course, this also meant no more discount coupons for us, but it kept Carleen from being so flustered and perplexed. And considering all that she does for the residents of Downtown, this was a very small price to pay! Amazingly, or maybe not so amazingly, Carleen suddenly found that nobody was coming to her asking for these change-of-address packets. I guess she's going to have to do her own research about where to go for that winter vacation.

Buying a car

When my car started to need more and more expensive repairs, and I worried constantly about breaking down on some deserted road in the dark of the night, I decided it was time to shop for a new vehicle. I thought back to my last experience of buying a car, which admittedly had been some time ago.

That time, it was more of an emergency purchase. It was January, I was living in Boston, and my engine froze up. I'm not well versed in how cars work, so I thought that a frozen-up engine must have been caused by the below-zero temperatures that day. However, as I was dismayed to learn, you can't simply thaw a frozen engine with a hair dryer or by parking it in a heated garage. No, when your car's engine freezes up, it's pretty much the end of the road, no pun intended. The problem had something to do with a hose under the hood that had cracked from

41

the cold. Because my car was old and not worth the cost of the repairs, I was going to have to buy a new one. I'd never done this by myself before, but I decided it could be a valuable learning experience.

The first thing was to select which kind of car to buy. And no, contrary to popular belief, women do not pick cars based on color. Fuel efficiency, low maintenance and a reasonable price – that's what's important. After doing considerable research online, I chose the Toyota RAV4.

Now I needed to figure out where to buy it and what the cost should be. Again, the Internet was a huge help. Not only did it explain "how to deal with car dealers," but it also helped me to determine what I should pay. I found a site where car dealers compete for your business, which at the time, was somewhat of a novelty. I typed in my e-mail address, the kind of car I wanted to buy and the region of the country I was living in. Within a short time, I had e-mails from several car dealers who wanted to offer me "a deal I couldn't refuse." After ascertaining the lowest price that anyone anywhere in the state was willing to offer, I borrowed a friend's car and drove to a nearby dealer, intent on paying that price. Car salesmen have a reputation for being slick and for being good at haggling. I decided I was going to be even better.

When I walked into the showroom, a salesman named Andre jumped up. I'm sure he thought that I, as an unaccompanied woman, would be an easy sell. Little did he know that I had done my homework and knew how to drive not only a car, but a hard bargain as well. I told

Andre that I was interested in a new RAV4 and was ready to buy it that evening. He smiled broadly and started punching numbers into his calculator.

"I can tell that you're a smart woman. And I like you," he said, looking me in the eye. "So I'm going to give you a really good deal. In fact, it's so good that I can't say it out loud." He scribbled a number on a piece of paper and pushed it across the desk toward me. I looked him back in the eye and put on my look of complete shock.

"What? No way!" I said. "I am not paying that much." Andre stood up and said he'd have to talk to his manager to see what he could do. When he came back several minutes later, he was beaming. Since it was getting late in the day, his manager had authorized him to knock some more off the price, he said proudly. He reached for the paper and wrote down a new number. I shook my head and once again put on my look of shock and dismay. "Still no deal," I said. After this game had gone on for several rounds, Andre was growing frustrated.

"How can we put you in a new car tonight?" he finally asked. "What price are you willing to pay?" I looked him in the eye. "It's such a good price that I can't say it out loud," I said calmly as I picked up the pencil and wrote down my price.

Although there was another discussion or two with the invisible manager and some whining about how he couldn't possibly make any money on this deal, Andre finally drew up the papers and I got my car -- at the price I intended to pay. Oh, yes, and in the color I wanted.

After all, there was no way I was going to settle for that ugly beige vehicle on the lot -- even if it meant waiting until the next day. Andre agreed to have a dealer elsewhere in the state ship the blue one I wanted.

Now, it's nearly ten years later, and I once again had to go through the pain of car shopping. Everyone here in town hates it when someone gets a new car. It's not that we're jealous. It's just that we get confused. You see, we all recognize each other by our cars. For instance, I know that when I see a dark grey Camry, it's Jane; if it's a maroon Nissan, it's Susan. The list goes on. Charlie used to drive a highly recognizable lime-green truck until he got that darn black one that looks like just about every other pickup in town. What were you thinking, Charlie? And now my ten-year old blue RAV4 – the only one in town – was history. I'd like to say that my new car is yellow or teal, or some color that would stand out. A car that you would see outside the general store, and immediately know that you could find me there. But the selection of car colors these days leaves a lot to be desired. The choices are basically white or black, silver or gold, maroon or dark grey. I settled on the dark grey.

I'm proud to say that I drove a hard bargain to get this new car. Though it required visits to four different dealers, I was able to drive the price down by nearly $3,000 between the first offer I received and the last. Finally, I was ready to sign on the dotted line. Before I could drive my new car off the lot, however, I had to listen to a tutorial, courtesy of Salesman Kurt, on all the car's bells and whistles – though come to think of it, he didn't actually show me how to operate useful accessories like the horn. He instructed me on how to turn on the air conditioning, tilt the steering wheel, open the windows, view my current miles per gallon, fold down the back seat and – most important of all – operate the onboard computer system. When Kurt was all done and climbed out of the car, I actually thought for a split second that the car might drive me home while I simply relaxed comfortably in the seat. However, I quickly realized that there are some things – though not many – that this car does *not* do on its own.

I still have a lot to learn about my new vehicle. For instance, Kurt didn't mention which side the gas tank was on or how to open it – which presented a slight problem the first time I needed to fill up with gas. I also don't know where the spare tire is, but hopefully I won't need it.

The other problem I'm having is finding my car when I park. It's not a problem here in town, of course, where there are only tiny parking lots and very few cars. But in large parking lots, my car just doesn't stand out in the sea of grey. I wonder if there's a setting on the car's computer that I could program to have the car honk out my name in Morse code every 30, 60 or 90 seconds – depending on my user preferences. I think I'll call Kurt and ask him. He did say I should just call if I have any questions, though he may already be regretting having made *that* statement since I now have him on Bluetooth voice-activated speed dial in my car. Good thing for him that cell coverage here is so spotty.

Winter driving

Almost every road in Downtown is steep and winding, making winter driving harrowing. I remember the time when I was at a party, and we could see out the window that the snow had started falling heavily. The topic naturally turned to winter driving. Kevin reported that his new car has a special button.

"It's magic," he said. "If the road is slick, I push the button, and it goes on auto pilot. I don't accelerate or brake. The car drives itself."

His wife piped in: "Let's clarify that, hon. The other night, you thought the car was driving itself, but we ended up in that ditch in front of Don's house. Remember? Do you think maybe your button isn't working right?"

I wanted to hear more about this magic button. I was thinking that perhaps my new car also has just such a button that I just haven't found yet. On my way *up* the hill to the party, an orange light had appeared on my dashboard that depicted a car swerving. I thought that it was a warning that my car was about to swerve off the road, which freaked me out. Now, six inches of snow later, I was going to have to drive *down* that same hill. And I was worried.

It seems that guys, however, don't get as concerned about slippery roads. They have everything under control when it comes to cars. Or so they say. And so the guys started offering advice about how to keep my car on the road driving home. They also told me exactly how I could come to a stop at the bottom of the hill and not slide out onto the main road, get hit by an oncoming plow, become airborne and land on (or in) the frozen lake. Did I mention that I always imagine the worst when driving on icy roads?

"So, here's a question," I said to those guys. "How do I turn off that annoying your-car-is-about-to-swerve-off-the-road light?" It is no help whatsoever. I think its only purpose is to make me nervous, which could lead to some bad decisions on my part.

"You can't turn it off," Tom told me. "It's a light, not a button. But," he added, "your car has many other knobs and buttons you can use. For instance, the radio knobs are a good choice. Turn them all the way up and just don't think about the ice."

The other guys also had advice – such as: "I say just grip the steering wheel tightly and make sure your seat belt is fastened." Or: "Put the car in neutral and coast. But not too fast."

"No, no, not neutral!" another guy advised. "You need to use low gear. Unless you're going around a hairpin turn. In that case, neutral is a good choice." The next tip was: "Start the car, put your foot on the brake and don't take it off until you're home."

By this point, I was totally confused about who I should listen to. And completely convinced that my trip home was not going to end well. "Like I told you," Kevin said, "you need a magic button." Tom disagreed: "No, no, no. You don't need any magic buttons. As I said, you just need a car with a loud radio."

And in a color you like," added our hostess, Marlene.

Wait! Even I know that car color is irrelevant. Marlene, however, is absolutely convinced that whenever there is any question related to a car, it all comes down to picking the right color.

The Downtown dump

People who live in urban areas – and I used to be one of them – put their trash out by the street and it miraculously disappears. In Downtown, however, I have to make my trash disappear myself – by taking it to the dump.

Actually, it's no longer known as the dump. It's now referred to as the transfer station. When I was a child, the dump was a place up a dirt road on the side of a mountain, where you could literally dump anything. In those days, we kids would pile into the back of our faded red Ford pickup truck, settling down right next to the garbage cans, and head for the dump. On hot days, the smell was particularly pungent, but we didn't care. The dump run was our weekly excitement. Nowadays, of course, kids have vastly different ideas about excitement. Not to mention that it's illegal to drive kids around in the back of an open truck. But back then, there were a lot fewer things that were illegal – including dumping all sorts of toxic waste.

At some point in the 1960s, Downtown decided to abandon their dump and move the site further up the mountain. I assume that they were probably told by the state government that they needed to clean up their act. A new location was selected, with a spectacular panoramic view stretching across multiple mountain ranges. A gated access road – christened Valley View Lane – was constructed, and the dump opened for business. Open is the operative word here. No longer could we dump at any hour and on any day of the week. There were specific opening times as well as restrictions on what we could and couldn't dump. And furthermore, we suddenly had to pay money to get rid of our trash.

With all these upgrades, it could, of course, no longer be referred to as the dump. It became the Sanitary Landfill. The concept was only slightly more environmentally correct. In principle, you weren't supposed to deposit things like used oil from your car, paint thinner, refrigerators, tires and the like. But if you were friendly with the attendant, you could throw pretty much anything over the bank into the huge hole in the side of the mountain. When the hole got full, a backhoe pushed mounds of dirt over it and dug a new hole.

There was a large shiny new shed and an attendant. Over the years, the shed filled up with items that people no longer wanted but couldn't bear to throw away: books (and the bookshelves to put them on), chairs, tables, lamps, barbecue grills, outdoor furniture, toys. The list goes on. A trip to the dump – which is how I will forever refer to it – was more like a trip to a second-hand store, where everything was free.

When the state decided that sanitary landfills were not really all that sanitary, they mandated that they all be converted to transfer stations. Suddenly you needed a college degree to know which trash went in which of the multitude of receptacles. When these fill up, a big truck comes along and transfers them somewhere else. Don't ask me where.

I still look forward to my weekly trip to the dump – though it's no longer in the back of a pickup truck. I often run into people I haven't seen in a while. And the attendants are always entertaining. There was Melanie, the bleached blonde who liked to dress in a slinky black cocktail dress with a long slit up the side. She had amazing tattoos and a significant weight problem. Then came Jeannie, who regaled us with tales of riding her horse into the next town to visit the bar. It made more sense to take her horse than her pickup truck, she said. That way, she could avoid any chance of getting arrested on a drunk-driving charge. As far as she knew, there were no laws against drunk riding.

When you live in a small town like Downtown, ordinary things make you happy: ice cube trays that are filled, trash cans that are empty and a strong sense of community. I feel like I know almost everyone in town. And the ones I don't know – well, I'll probably meet them at some point during a visit to the dump.

Trapper Zeke

Here in Downtown, I accept that I must share my property with wildlife: chipmunks, squirrels, fox, raccoons, deer and other critters – some of whom I don't really want to know about. For instance, skunks. But a skunk is not something to be ignored. So, when I discovered one living beside my house, everyone told me, "Call Trapper Zeke."

When Zeke showed up a few days later, I showed him the hole where I thought the skunk had taken up residence. He stroked his beard and looked skeptical. It might be difficult to trap, Zeke told me, since this isn't the only entry (or exit) for him. But he proceeded to set up his have-a-heart trap, a metal cage that catches the animal without hurting it. He built a kind of makeshift tunnel outside the hole. Zeke explained that the skunk would smell the bait and the horrific-smelling liquid that he referred to as the lure and be led right into the trap. As one wall of the tunnel, he used a metal sign that he had brought along. It read "No Trespassing."

"Do you think that's smart, this "No Trespassing" sign?" I teased. "We *want* the skunk to go into the cage, right?" Zeke looked at me briefly, then continued his work. "Ma'am," he said rather matter-of-factly. "Skunks can't actually read." At this point, I thought that he must take me for a complete idiot. Or maybe he was just as much of a tease as I am. Turns out it was the latter.

I had never met a trapper before, and I was eager to learn about their trade. I started asking questions, and he seemed pleased that I was interested in the art of trapping — and not just some squeamish city-slicker who couldn't deal with wild animals living so close by.

Zeke said that he's been trapping since he was a kid. His explanation of just how much he loves trapping was a gem: "Ever seen a dog hangin' out the car window, tongue a-dangling and ears pinned back by the wind? Is there any happier being than that? That's me when I'm trapping." It gets him up and out on cold winter mornings, he added. "I used to hunt. But when you hunt, you might wake up, look at the thermometer, and decide to go back to sleep. With trapping, you have to be out there every day, checking your traps. It wouldn't be humane to leave the animals in the trap any longer than necessary."

Zeke explained that there are two kinds of trapping licenses: nuisance trapping and commercial trapping. "I guess all skunk trapping is nuisance trapping," I said. "They're certainly a big nuisance. And you don't see many women rushing to buy skunk coats."

But this wasn't always the case, according to Zeke. Skunk used to be passed off as Alaskan sable and it was a prized fur – until the early 1950s, when the courts ruled that customers must be informed if something had skunk parts in it. That put a quick end to the skunk trade.

We then got onto the topic of beaver, of which we also have plenty here in these parts. Every schoolchild here knows that the early American settlers were always out trapping beaver. I never really thought too much about what they did with it. But, of course, Zeke knew. They shipped it to Europe, where it was turned into felt for hats, including the popular top hat. When silk hats came into vogue in the 19th century, it was very good news for the beavers. It was also good for the hatters, many of whom had become mad over time, poisoned by the mercury used in felt processing. Hence, the term mad hatter.

Who would have thought that my encounter with Zeke would be so educational? Now, you want to know, did we catch the skunk? Well, no. But we did catch a raccoon. They can also be very pesky and clever enough to open a trashcan and strew trash all around your property. In the end, I thought to myself, catching one raccoon, or even one skunk, really wasn't going to solve any problems for me. There would always be more. I'll just have to learn to live with my wild neighbors.

A better mousetrap

As a single woman, I have found that there are numerous advantages to living alone: I can play my music as loudly as I want. I can yell at the television when some politician makes a stupid remark – which seems to happen with increasing frequency these days. I don't have to let anyone know where I'm going when I leave the house or when I plan to return.

But alas, I suddenly realized one fall day that I was no longer living alone. I had a housemate. In fact, several housemates. They were not paying any rent, but at least they were as quiet as a mouse. In fact, that's just what they were. When I first noticed signs of mice in my garage, I was not too concerned. I figured there wasn't much damage to be done in there. But when they moved into my living space, that's when they had gone too far. The first sign of them was the chewed-up roll of toilet paper in my bathroom. If they were that close to my bedroom, I thought, how long would it take before they became comfortable about visiting me in my bed at night? This will never do!

I immediately headed to the hardware store to purchase mousetraps. These, I discovered, come in a wide variety. There is the old-fashioned wooden kind, which I'm not fond of. It's not that I care what they do to the mice, but I do care what they might do to my finger if I set the trap wrong. There are also the sticky traps. The mouse walks onto it and is stuck for life. Much as I hate these mice, I don't want to be inhumane. So, I opted for the plastic snap traps, which offer an instant kill.

The next question was what to use for bait. I learned from my Internet research that mice love peanut butter. I wasn't sure whether they prefer crunchy or smooth, but I opted for the smooth. My neighbor, who is a foodie, told me that he had caught 34 mice in the preceding two weeks, using a gourmet brand of peanut butter. When I told him about my lack of success, he launched into an explanation of why the PRICE-LESS brand of peanut butter I was using would never work. Wow, who knew that mice would be so picky?

And that leads me to the next problem. When I checked my traps, I often found that the peanut butter had been licked clean but there was no sign of any mouse in the trap. Apparently, I not only had a smart phone and a smart TV, but also smart mice.

Another neighbor told me that he makes his own trap out of a bucket. Using a piece of wood, he creates a ramp leading up to the rim of the bucket. He then puts a rod through a soda can, smears peanut butter on the far end of the can and positions the rod across the top of the bucket. When the unsuspecting mouse moseys up the ramp and steps on the can on his way to a peanut butter snack, the can starts spinning and the mouse gets deposited in the bucket. Now that's what I call inventing a better mousetrap!

Depending on how humane you are, you might have put just a few inches of water in the bucket so the mouse can take a swim. Or you might decide to use an empty bucket, in which case you would just release the captured mouse outside. Of course, there's no guarantee that the little critter won't just come right back into your house looking for some more peanut butter. But then again, now you know how to trap it.

PRICE-LESS

The fact that Downtown is so far removed from nearly everything is great for those of us who love solitude, hate crowds and abhor the thought of sitting in traffic. But the downside is that it's also far removed from things we would really like to have – like a real grocery store.

Well, okay there is a big discount grocery/department store called PRICE-LESS half an hour away in the next town. The food selection is often fairly limited, particularly when it comes to produce. Meals need to be based on what they happen to have in stock on the day you go shopping. And I've given up on trying to prepare anything that requires ingredients that could be considered even slightly out of the ordinary. If you want soda, chips, frozen pizza, ice cream or any one of 84 varieties of cereal (all fortified with essential minerals and vitamins, of course), you're in luck. On the other hand, if you're looking for something like red cabbage or blue cheese, you may have to rethink your menu plan.

Enough for the grocery department. Let's move on to the clothing. I don't believe that any item in the store costs more than $14.99. Now, I'm not the type who shops in high-end boutiques. And I like to get a deal as much as the next person. But I find that the prices are often better at the church thrift store down the street – higher quality items, albeit gently used, and generally priced at $3.00 or less.

Now let's move on to the jewelry section. It's all costume jewelry, of course. I have nothing against costume jewelry, but somehow it just seems plain wrong to see someone put an engagement ring in a shopping cart along with a hunting rifle, oil for the car, a 24-pack of beer and toilet paper.

PRICE-LESS can actually be a good source of entertainment, particularly in the winter when not much else is going on. Some friends and I once had a contest to see who could put together the most outrageous outfit (including clothing, purse, shoes and jewelry) for the least amount of money. Oh yes, and you had to be willing to wear it out in public for an entire evening. Of course, 'out in public' in Downtown simply means going over to a friend's house. Or the dump.

I once heard someone in the check-out line reminiscing with her girlfriend about the time several years ago that they had stayed overnight at PRICE-LESS on

Thanksgiving night, waiting for the Black Friday sale to start. Moving into a PRICE-LESS isn't all that far-fetched since it's open 24 hours a day, seven days a week. And you have everything you need right there: folding chairs, sleeping bags, pajamas, clean underwear, junk food, beer, toothpaste – and even a bathroom. If you're bored, you can wander over to the electronics section and watch TV, grab a board game from the toy department or ride around the store on a bicycle from the sporting goods section. I'm not sure that anyone would even conclude that you were living in the store since I often see people shopping there in the middle of the day in their pajamas. And, as far as I know, they aren't living there!

Whose birthday is it?

One thing that all of us in Downtown have in common is that we all have birthdays. This got me thinking about something. How would you like to have your birthday moved to a different date? I'm not talking here about moving it to a different year as some movie stars have been known to do in order to shave years off their age. No, at issue here is moving birthdays to a different day of the month, so that bank and government employees can enjoy a three-day weekend. This is what happened to two of America's most famous presidents – George Washington and Abraham Lincoln – when their birthdays were quite simply moved to the third Monday of February some years back. There was no need to ask them if they objected since they had been dead for years. They probably wouldn't have raised much fuss even if they *had* been alive since, as we all know, they made great sacrifices for the good of the country; and presumably having to sacrifice their true birthdays for the benefit of the country's civil servants would have been a no-brainer for them.

When I was a kid in Downtown, we celebrated Lincoln's birthday on February 12 and Washington's on February 22. I can still remember those dates – after all, what better way to burn historical dates into kids' heads than to associate them with a day off from school? The trade-off for the day off was that we had to write papers and take tests about both Lincoln and Washington to help us understand their greatness. We learned that both of these men had worked hard, were honest and sacrificed much for their country. We were taught that Honest Abe, as he was known, had schooled himself, studying long into the evenings by the light of his oil lamp. The clear message here was that we should be grateful that we had teachers and electric lights, and that, with hard work and perseverance, we might also one day become president. Well, actually, that last message was directed only at the boys in the class.

Washington, the first president of the United States, was also a very honest guy. We were told that when George was a young boy, his father gave him a hatchet, which he promptly used to chop down a cherry tree in his back yard. Soon thereafter, his dad stumbled upon his favorite tree, lying there on the ground, and was very angry. Personally, I could imagine that mom might have been pretty angry at dad for giving little George a hatchet in the first place. When his dad asked who had chopped down the tree, George said, "Father, I cannot tell a lie. I did it." As the story goes, the father was so happy that his son had told the truth that he hugged him and was no longer angry. Although the message they were trying to teach us with this legend might seem pretty clear, it never really worked for me. My parents were usually still pretty angry even after I admitted that I had done something naughty. But back to George and his legend: It turns out that the whole cherry tree story actually isn't even true; it was made up to teach kids that they should always tell the truth. Go figure.

The purse

When September arrives, many women start thinking about transferring their worldly belongings to a different purse. After all, according to a hard and fast fashion rule, it is absolutely forbidden to carry a white purse or wear white shoes after Labor Day. And though my purse is really not all that white after all it's been through over the summer, the time had come to switch to an autumn color. And, since there's not much else to do on a cold, rainy Sunday afternoon in Downtown, I rooted around in the depths of my closet and found a lovely pumpkin-colored bag that I'd forgotten about. Perfect!

Here's what I *hate* about changing purses: I always aim to transfer only the bare essentials – in order not to create clutter in the new bag – but how do I decide what's essential and what's not? And here's what I *love* about changing purses: finding treasures – items that were deemed non-essential and stayed in the old purse when it was put away. The pumpkin bag contained not only an old tube of lipstick (yikes! I really wore that color?) and dried out pens, but also scraps of paper with notes I'd made – the name of a book someone had recommended, a must-see movie title, a couple of ideas for a novel I might write one day. I pulled out a silver barrette bought on a trip to Arizona a decade and a half ago. The clip is broken, and my hair is now too short for a barrette. But I paused for a moment to let the images from that trip flash through my mind. Digging deeper, I pulled out my good-luck coin – a two-pfennig piece I had received in change at the airport on the day I moved from Germany to the U.S. How did I deem *that* non-essential? Next, a business card with the name Joe McNally on it. Is he that guy I met at a conference in Chicago some years back? As I recall, we came up with an idea, over some adult beverages, for a can't-miss business venture that would make us millions. We promised to keep in touch. We didn't. If we had, and if I'd kept the two-pfennig piece close to me, would I be a millionaire now? Maybe. Maybe not.

By this point, I was totally into my trip down memory lane. The rain was still pouring down outside, my 'purse action' was completed, and it seemed like a great time to move onto that carton of books in the same closet. After all, someone from my high school class had recently contacted me through Facebook, and I had been meaning to look up his photo in my high school yearbook, which I knew was in that box. I pulled it out and started reading the hand-written comments from classmates: *"To a sweet girl."* *"To a nice girl."* *"To a good kid."* Most are inane. But not all. *"To that lovely girl, who without her help, I would never have met Mr. Joseph J. Lyons face to face."* Mr. Lyons was the Assistant Principal in charge of discipline – and nobody ever wanted to be sent to *his* office. Was I really that mean to this fellow who signed his name Frank? Next, I looked at the list of activities next to my photo. What was I thinking when I joined the Future Nurses of America? And I had totally forgotten that I played the clarinet in the marching band. Our band wasn't really very good. In fact, we could never figure out how to play our instruments and march at the same time. So, we would march into a formation, then stop and play a song. And since I nearly failed science classes in college, how did I ever get into the biology honor society? It also says that I won the heather award. I wonder what that was for.

My yearbook, like my old purse, contained so many nuggets that sparked memories of people and places long forgotten. How lucky I am, I thought, to have all these treasures stored away for a rainy day.

Friends

Although I have lived in a few cities and suburbs as well as in Downtown during my lifetime, I have always found that I have a much wider circle of friends in Downtown than anywhere else. On my desk, I have a tiny book entitled simply 'Friends.' I bought it years ago as a gift, but found that I just couldn't part with it. It's a collection of quotations about friendship – some beautiful, some sentimental, some humorous. Occasionally, when I'm sitting at my desk, I'll pick up the book and read a few of the quotations. Each in its own way reminds me of how special my friends are – each in *their* own way. Take Megan, for instance. *"There are some friends you know you will have for the rest of your life. You're welded together by love, trust, respect or loss – or... simple embarrassment."*

In the early 1970s, Megan and I were young, carefree and working in Washington, D.C. One evening – most likely under the influence of the cheap wine we liked to drink – we decided we should quit our jobs and go to Europe. Amazingly, when we awoke the next day, we still liked the idea. So we gave notice at our jobs, bought backpacks, hiking boots and youth hostel passes, and made plane reservations for early September.

To make our money go as far as possible, our plan was to hitch-hike, stay in youth hostels and buy food in grocery stores. Europe on $5 a day was our goal. We hitched our first ride with a couple of American soldiers on motorcycles. They were eager to show us the sights – which involved a wine festival on the Mosel. Suffice it to say that the evening did not end well for our soldier friends, who had their drivers' licenses confiscated by the local police. We vowed to be more discriminating in choosing our rides from then on.

For seven months, we hitchhiked through Europe – north to Scandinavia and south to Turkey. We met some wonderful people – like Nicholas who invited us to stay in his home on the Greek island of Kalymnos for as long as we wanted. And we met some characters – like the two Bulgarian truck drivers who invited us to live with them forever in the back of their truck. Of course, with the language barrier, we couldn't be sure that's what they really said! Or the guys in Istanbul who… But those are stories for another day.

When our money ran out in the spring, Megan returned to Washington, and I settled in Germany. Yes, it had something to do with a dashing German man that I had met. And her decision had something to do with a college boyfriend who was suddenly back in the picture and begging her to come home. Staying in touch with Megan wasn't easy – back in the days before e-mail and Skype. But we managed. Today we live on opposite coasts of the U.S. We rarely get together. But when we do, it's like we're – well, you know – old friends. There's no substitute for a friend who has known you through so many stages of your life – the good, the bad, the exciting and even the boring. A friend who knows what makes you laugh, and who or what has made you cry. It's the quintessential comfort zone.

Fair game

I consider myself to be courageous, which means occasionally living outside my comfort zone. Perhaps that's why, when my 10-year-old grandson Josh was visiting me in Downtown recently, I decided to take him to a fair that had set up its temporary quarters in the next town. At the first ring-toss booth, Josh was absolutely certain that he could win that five-foot tall tiger because, he told me, he was a real expert at tossing rings. And, as I soon discovered, he was also a real expert at tossing the bull. As it turns out, you could buy one ring for 50 cents, or three for $1. But if you wanted a real bargain (I am using the term loosely here), you could get 20 rings for $5. Of course, Josh said, we should go for the bargain. I thought about arguing with him that an expert ring-tosser like himself would only need one ring -- and would land the tiger on the first throw. But I knew that this was not an argument I would win. So I pulled out the $5 bill and put it on the counter. 20 rings later, he still didn't have the tiger. "But now I see how to do this," Josh said. "Let's buy another 20 rings and I'll get it this time." This could turn out to be a really expensive tiger.

Well, he never did get the tiger. But there were plenty more places where we could spend our (or my) money. Josh was equally unsuccessful at the next several booths. Then he saw a sign that said, "Everyone is a winner!" This was the right booth for him, he decided. It didn't say what you would win. But after all, paying $5 to win a $1 keychain is worth it, right? You're a winner. And who can turn down the 100 percent certainty of being a winner? Not Josh! And thus also not I.

My wallet was getting thinner. And then we spotted it. The one booth that Josh positively could not pass up. The goldfish booth. All you had to do was toss a ping pong ball into just ONE of the many fishbowls and you could go home with your very own goldfish. Josh was sure he could do it. By now, I had a much better understanding of his aim, even if he did not. After all, I reminded myself, he can't hit the toilet, so the chances of him hitting an even smaller bowl are slim. So I stepped right up, as the carnival barker told us to do, and laid my money on the table. Just $5 for an entire bucket of balls. Bucket sounds big. Truth be told, this was more like a dish, holding about 10 balls. Josh was absolutely certain that he was soon to be the proud owner of his very own goldfish. But getting a ping pong ball into a bowl turned out to be a feat too difficult to master. As we got down to the last ball, I was secretly relieved that I would not have to explain to his parents why I let him come home with a goldfish. But wait! It turns out that this was another one of those everyone-is-a-winner booths. Josh was going to win the goldfish after all. You see, it was the last day of the fair, and obviously this guy didn't want to have to bring all these goldfish home with him, so he was giving them away like it was Christmas. We probably could have gotten five of them if we had just asked. So, he was a winner, too, since we took the fish off his hands. Everyone is a winner. Except, of course, the goldfish.

"You're a winner!" he told Josh as he scooped a goldfish into a plastic bag filled with water and handed it over. The look of pure delight (not to mention surprise) on Josh's face made the entire fair experience one to treasure. No amount of money can buy that joy. And, I might add that there was another advantage to this little win. Josh decided that we could not spend another second at the fair. No, we had to rush home to get the fish into a proper tank because living in a plastic bag was not a good experience for this darling little creature, which he promptly named Goldie. As an aside, Josh's sister Lexi is somewhat more creative with names. Her fish are called Gil and Finn, and she even named her Christmas tree Cris.

But I digress. Back to Josh. And Goldie. When we arrived home, it should come as no surprise that the rest of the family was somewhat less thrilled than Josh about his new fish. Fortunately, I had an old glass bowl that was quickly designated as Goldie's new home.

While Lexi cleaned up the bowl and older sisters Gabby and Brie tried to figure out what to feed Goldie, Josh decided to run off to play with a friend. So much for fatherhood and responsibility. No matter. He's the birthday boy. We didn't have any fish food in the house, but we learned during a quick online search that "goldfish owners can boil or microwave leafy vegetables like lettuce and spinach, and even peas" and feed them to the goldfish. We started taking bets about how long Goldie would survive – even if Josh was willing to make the ultimate sacrifice of sharing some of his spinach with Goldie. I was the most skeptical. "An hour," I said. Brie was more optimistic. "Oh, come on. I give it at least a day." Suddenly Lexi appeared and matter-of-factly stated, "The fish is dead." Well, I definitely won that bet, I announced. Remember, everyone is a winner.

I admit that I was a bit worried that Josh might have a meltdown when he got back and realized that Goldie was no longer among the living. I had a speech all prepared to help ease his pain. But it turned out to be unnecessary. "Oh, well," he said. "Yup," I told him. "Just think of the advantages. Now you'll get to eat all your spinach yourself!"

Thanksgiving

Think about the origins of Thanksgiving, when the Pilgrims put on a huge feast to thank the Native Americans for their help in settling into 'their' new country. Apparently, it wasn't yet clear to those Native Americans that the arrival of the white settlers wasn't necessarily going to be all that advantageous for them.

Today the holiday has evolved into a time for extended families to travel great distances to get together with people that they wouldn't necessarily choose to have dinner with otherwise. And Downtown is no exception. My typical Thanksgiving Day starts off early in the morning when the turkey gets stuffed and put in the oven. Over the many years that I have hosted

Thanksgiving gatherings, I can tell you that nearly any disaster that can occur has occurred – from the power going out in the middle of roasting the turkey, to pies being dropped on the floor as they come out of the oven, to candles being knocked over and setting the tablecloth on fire. But let's not focus on the negative. Let's assume that everyone is getting along, thanks to lots of Bloody Marys, that the turkey isn't totally dried out, the vegetables didn't get burned and that Aunt Emily actually remembered to bring the mashed potatoes this year.

After dinner, and after everyone says – as they do every year – "I can't believe I ate so much," the next phase begins. This entails either moving into the den with copious amounts of beer to watch a football game OR making a mad dash to the stores for some major shopping. The choice generally depends on whether you are male or female. Of course, 'going shopping' for people in Downtown entails about a one-hour drive to the nearest mall. And since it's such a long drive, the women tend to carpool. After all, getting there is half the fun.

In former times, the day after Thanksgiving was the year's biggest shopping day, known as Black Friday because the huge sales enabled businesses to climb out of the red and into the black. Today, the sales already start on Thursday afternoon. Stores advertise computers, fridges, big screen tv sets and other big-ticket items at ridiculously low prices. There is no mention of the fact that they only have one of each in stock, but people are wise to this and thus get in line hours before the stores open. As the store opening hours grow earlier and earlier, some people now skip Thanksgiving dinner in order to get in line. And although this might be good for women who are shopping for clothing and want to squeeze into that smaller size, it's not that great for family together-time.

Very late in the evening, the women return home, their cars laden with stuff. It's of course either not the stuff they set out to buy – since that wasn't actually available – or it *is* that stuff, but not at the sale price. Meanwhile, hopefully the guys' team won the football game so they're in a good mood – because they are going to have to carry all that merchandise into their houses. And the kids, who have been at home with the guys (how much supervision do you think they got?) and have a sugar high from all the desserts, are running wild. All those items that the Moms bought to put away for Christmas presents? The kids see them and start ripping open the boxes, demanding that Dad hook up the new TV, connect the new x-box and load all the software onto the new computer – RIGHT NOW. After all that beer, Dad isn't really in shape to do any of the above. In fact, it's good if he can just get all those boxes into the house without dropping them. Ah, it looks like the true meaning of Thanksgiving in today's world might be that we are thankful when it's all over and we can finally fall thankfully into bed.

Home moaner's manual

Who doesn't have a ton of things around the house that need to be repaired? To help with these projects, everyone needs Home Moaner's Manual. And you're in luck – I just happen to have one for you.

I should let you know that I am the quintessential tool person. Despite the fact that I am a single woman, I have so many tools that I don't even know what some of them are supposed to be used for. Many stem from kindly souls from around Downtown who have offered to help me with a project and then left some tools behind – perhaps accidentally, perhaps in the hopes that I wouldn't have to call them ever again. I do know what a hammer looks like, as well as a screwdriver. Once we get into the wrench department, things get more complicated. I'm not quite sure why anyone would need as many wrenches as I have acquired over the years. Last summer, I bought a really expensive wrench at the request of someone who had offered to help me remove the engine from my wood chipper (yes, I really do have a wood chipper and no, I don't remember why we decided to remove the engine). The project didn't end well, and that friend hasn't been back. Home Moaner's Manual tip #1: Make sure you have lots of friends, since most of them only extend an offer to help once.

Here's tip #2: Don't hesitate to ask anyone who drops by for assistance. My theory is that most guys love to play the role of aiding a damsel in distress. Let's say your lawn mower won't start. When the UPS or FedEx guy comes by the next time, just ask him if he knows anything about lawn mowers. Since most guys would give up their right arm and first-born son rather than admit that they can't fix something, of course they're going to offer to help. Unfortunately, these delivery guys have now gotten wise to my ways and I rarely see them anymore. The first sign I had that they were avoiding me was when they started quietly placing my package on the porch without ringing the doorbell. I then installed a driveway alarm so that I could hear them when they drove in. But the next thing I knew, they were parking their truck on the main road and walking in my driveway.

I was thinking that I might need to delete tip #2 from the manual – but I came up with a backup plan. I call the cable company to report that my television isn't working properly and ask them to please send someone to check it out. This tactic has served me well when I've needed help with something like moving furniture. After all, there he is, right in the living room when I need that table moved.

And finally, one more way to get help is to invite a friend over. Break out the single malt scotch before getting around to the topic at hand. This tactic can be a bit tricky since, although the friend might not be able to refuse to help with the project after you've plied him with your best spirits, he also may no longer be capable of successfully completing the project.

Now that the UPS and FedEx guys are leaving my packages at the Post Office, now that the cable guy seems to be able to fix all my cable issues remotely, and now that my friends all tell me that they've given up drinking when I invite them over for a cocktail, I'm going to have to come up with some new tactics for getting help with my projects. Friends have occasionally suggested that I might want to look for a live-in boyfriend. One who is handy with tools. But before I resort to that, I have a few more tactics in my toolbox.

Telecommuting

I used to work in the city. But when I moved to Downtown, I became a remote employee, a telecommuter. It would be hard to beat my workspace here in Downtown. My morning commute is from my kitchen to my couch, coffee cup in hand. As I wait for my laptop to boot up, my view is of the lake – and occasionally a deer grazing on the path out front.

But before you turn green with envy about this cushy work environment, I will admit that there are some – admittedly, not many – disadvantages. For instance, I can't sit out on my deck during a conference call. A boat buzzing by or pesky crows squawking overhead are a dead giveaway that 'someone' on the call is not sequestered in a cubicle like everyone else. I've also learned some etiquette: When people ask where I'm calling in from, I no longer say, "From my deck beside the lake."

But perhaps the most important thing I've learned is how to get out of participating in those deadly conference calls. It's not that I mind working, but I want to do it on my own time. And that's not at 1 pm on a spectacular, sunny day – which is when clients invariably want to schedule calls. I prefer to work early in the morning or in the evening so I can get out and enjoy the day. After all, that's why I live here. But I'm not completely inflexible. On rainy days, I can make myself available any time.

So, what's the trick to getting clients to accept the fact that I'm not always available for a call? I've developed a list of reasons to explain why they'll have to reschedule the call or send me an email with the info. So, just in case any of you find yourself in need of excuses – whoops, I mean reasons – I'm happy to share some with you for the upcoming spring and summer.

If you're planning a hike, your response to a meeting request is, "Sorry, but I have another high-level meeting at that time."

If you've been invited to go sailing, tell the client, "I have another commitment, but I should be able to sail through that and be available later in the afternoon."

When the forecast is for sunny, hot weather, and you don't feel like working too hard that week, you say, "I'm just trying to keep my head above water at the moment, so I'm not going to be able to take on that project."

Would you rather be out paddleboarding than stuck on some call? Here's what you say: "I've got a lot to skim through this morning. Can we do the call later in the day?"

And if you just want to hang out at the beach for the day, taking an occasional dip to cool off, you tell the client, "I'm about to dive into something that will probably take most of the day."

So, now that you're armed with excuses, all you need to do is to find an employer who will let you telecommute!

Nothing gained

When the days start turning warmer in the spring, I start to sweat the fact that, unless I win the lottery and can purchase my own Caribbean island, I might have to soon appear in public in a bathing suit. Time to take action. The ads for the fitness center in our neighboring town promised me I could "Get in Shape Fast!!" Okay, it can't hurt, I thought. WRONG!! In fact, it not only can hurt, it does hurt -- in places I didn't even know I had.

After signing up for membership, I was told to return the next Tuesday at noon for an "entry-level test." The sheet of instructions read: "No alcohol or cigarettes for 24 hours before the test, no coffee or tea the day of the test and no food whatsoever for the 6 hours preceding the test. Bring a towel and wear something loose-fitting and comfortable." Yeah, right! The reason I had decided to join the club in the first place was because everything I owned was no longer loose-fitting or comfortable.

Tuesday arrived and I was up early eating breakfast. I'd rather sacrifice a few hours of sleep than a meal, and as long as I finished breakfast by 5 am, I'd be okay. I arrived at the gym, and was greeted by my trainer Joe who tested my fat and muscle levels and then designed a program of exercises aimed at attacking the problem zones of my body. In my case, these tend to start just below the neck and end at the ankles. I was shown machines for the chest and for the back, a machine for the upper arms, machines for the waist, the stomach, the hips and the rear end, machines for the inner thighs, the outer thighs, the backs and fronts of the thighs and the calves. "And once you've finished exercising on the machines," Joe said, "then you do at least 20 minutes of cardiovascular training on the stair stepper, the treadmill or the bicycle."

The cancellation clause in the membership contract was starting to look pretty attractive at this point. But these fitness clubs are cagey. They install mirrors -- curved in a way that makes everyone look 20 pounds heavier -- on every wall. Seeing myself in those funhouse mirrors made me realize that I better stick with the regimen. By the way, this same mirror company has also figured out how to produce mirrors with a reverse curve, which they market to department stores for their fitting rooms so that every dress you try on makes you look slim and svelte.

After learning about all the exercise machines, I decided to try out an exercise class. I settled on one called the "P class." The "P" stands for *problem zones* such as the tummy and hips. In point of fact, it is actually a secret designation for *pain class*. Sit ups with your feet in the air, sit ups with your legs wrapped around your neck, sit ups with your knees tucked behind your ears and then, without a moment's rest, 500 leg raises (on each side, mind you) with weights balanced on your outer thigh. I decided that this "P" class was not for me since it would simply cause me pain and problems. I wouldn't be able to move the next day.

As I was leaving the gym, I saw a sign that read, "Nothing ventured, nothing gained." Aha, I thought to myself. Now, there's a simple solution to prevent weight gain. I simply won't venture anything.

Looking for
a few good men

Before I moved to Downtown, I made several other moves, which generally included finding a new job, a new place to live and new friends – in short, starting an entirely new life. It didn't take me long to discover that this feat was amazingly similar to my decision as a foolish young girl to jump out of an airplane at 3,000 feet with a parachute strapped to my back. I simply closed my eyes, took a deep breath and made the plunge – without ever looking back.

Needless to say, I survived these leaps into the unknown. In fact, I like to think that I am infinitely wiser and humbler for having lived through these experiences. And although you the reader might think that hurtling through space at death-defying speed, waiting to see if your parachute will indeed open, is as scary as it gets, I'm here to tell you that it pales in comparison to the anxiety you will feel should you ever decide to re-enter the dating scene.

When I moved to Boston, at the age of 45 and freshly divorced, I was perfectly content to sit at home on Saturday night with a good book and a glass of wine. After a few months of that, however, I started thinking that if a smart witty good-looking hunk who also happens to be a great conversationalist dropped by, he just might be able to entice me to go out to dinner with him. It didn't take me long to realize that this phantom guy was not sitting by his phone trying to muster the courage to ask me out. In fact, it occurred to me that I was actually going to have to make some effort to seek out members of the opposite sex.

Once I came to this realization, I began researching the options for finding available guys. The first path I went down was something which I could do from the comfort and safety of my own living room couch – answering singles ads online. There were columns upon columns of guys just waiting to meet Ms. Right. But have you ever actually looked closely at any of those ads?

WM (which is "personals" talk for white male) 52, lives with three animals – my dog, my cat and my brother. I'm no animal but my bite is worse than my bark. Let's howl together!

Or how about this one: *Catch me while I last. Handsome, athletic, intelligent. Seeking elegant and voluptuous SWF (single white female) who knows perfection when she sees it and wants me all to herself.*

Finally, I saw one that looked like he might be worth contacting: *Nice easygoing guy. Loves dining out, traveling, the city and the country, long talks, quiet times and good books. Looking for that special someone who is passionate yet gentle and whose intellectual capital earns a high rate of interest.* Hey! At least this guy sound intriguing, I thought. But, as luck would have it, just as I was about to hit 'send,' I noticed that I had somehow wandered into the Men Looking for Men section.

Oh, now here's a live wire: *Handsome guy, 6' tall, home, car, financially independent. My bags are packed and I have my traveling boots on. Seeking woman who has some life left, is not waiting to die, like some I've met. Age 83, but looks 79.*

I showed this to a friend at work who was convinced that it was her grandfather, apparently looking to cheat on grandma!

Okay, so maybe these guys all just have a hard time expressing themselves, I thought. I should give a couple of them a chance. I'll contact them and see what happens. The first guy who responded was either excruciatingly nervous or was having a really bad time adjusting to a serious caffeine habit. "Hi, my name's Tom and I like to dance, that's what I do all the time is dance, you know, any kind of music is just fine to dance to, cajun, beebop, rap, it doesn't matter, I'm just always dancing, even when I'm just walking down the street, I'm dancing, I'm moving to the tunes which are always in my head…"

By the time he finally paused briefly to take a breath, I knew that this guy was definitely more in the category of nightmare than dream man. Seeing the perfect way out, I quickly interjected that I hate dancing. He didn't miss a beat. "Doesn't matter because you can watch me dance, I love it when other people watch me dance…" Just listening to him was exhausting. No, I most definitely did NOT want to meet him for a cup of coffee or watch him dance.

The other guys who responded were all just as bad, each in his own individual annoying way. One was a doctor who most likely had undergone some coaching on how to talk to women from some well-meaning (but equally clueless) friends. After several minutes of really dull conversation, he suddenly said, "Now I have to tell you something funny." The "something" was the fact that he had bent down that morning to pick up something he had dropped, and his pants had split at the seam. While he was guffawing about his own joke, I made some feeble excuse and quickly hung up the phone. Time to give up on the online dating and move on to some other avenue of meeting available men.

Seeing an ad in the paper for a singles club, I mustered my courage and called the number. The woman who answered the phone told me that a meeting was scheduled for the next week, and that it would be a pot luck dinner. I should bring a dessert. I arrived at the site of the meeting – the church beside the firehouse on the main street of the town in question. I parked my car and – with pineapple upside down cake in hand – followed some others into the church. We all went downstairs and into a meeting room where we were greeted and given name tags. "You're new, aren't you?" the man handing out name tags said to me. "Welcome! And I see you brought something to eat. That's great!" He seemed a bit surprised, actually. It was then that I noticed that I seemed to be the only one who had remembered that this was a potluck dinner. There was no other food in sight.

I sat down at a table and began chatting with some of the other guests. Suddenly, a man walked to the front of the room and began to speak. "Hello," he said. "My name is Mike, and I'm an alcoholic."

I looked around. I was in an AA meeting. Well, at least I hadn't brought a rum cake, I thought to myself. In any case, I definitely needed to make my exit. Not because I have anything against alcoholics, but simply because I was starving and needed to get to that other meeting where there would hopefully be some food and – of secondary importance at this point -- some singles.

I then discovered that there was another church on the other side of the firehouse. Again, I followed some people as they went inside. And again, I was greeted at the door by someone handing out name tags. Because I was a newcomer, I was given a blue name tag. The old timers all had red ones. And I do mean old timers. As I looked around the room, I discovered that I was the youngest one there – by at least 20 years. Harriet, a woman with a blue name tag, struck up a conversation with me, telling me that she was newly single and very nervous. "They have such wonderful music here," she said as Harry the "disk jockey" inserted a Mel Tormé cassette. Yes, they were still using cassettes. "I like it when you can understand the words to the songs," she added.

Noticing that Joe – a red-tagged old timer – was moving slyly toward us, I politely moved on to allow him to focus on Harriet, who was decidedly a better match for him. I next found myself talking with two women – one with a blue tag and one with a red tag. Red was explaining to blue, "It's very easy to mingle. You simply walk up to anyone, and most of them will talk to you."

"Most?" I asked innocently.

"Well," she replied, "all of the men will most definitely talk to you. And most of the women will, too."

"Most?" I asked again.

"Honey," she said, "you have to understand that some of the women are the jealous type. If they've had their eye on a particular guy for quite some time, they don't like it when new competition comes onto the field."

A picture flashed through my mind of a pack of senior ladies going at it in a knock-down-drag-out brawl over a silver-haired Romeo. My mother always told me 'pick your battles' and this was one battle that I was definitely *not* going to pick.

During dinner, I sat next to Jack, who turned out to be a collector. Aha, I thought. At least this could lead to some interesting conversation about art and antiques. He had recently moved east from Colorado and was lamenting the fact that he had had to put most of his collection in storage. He was hoping to find a larger place soon so that he could have it all shipped to him.

I conjured up rooms filled with lovely antique furnishings just waiting for him to find that perfect Victorian mansion. Wrong! When we got down to the details of exactly what it is that he collects, I discovered that it was neither art nor antiques. He collects old cars. But not Bentleys or Model Ts. No, rather they are junk cars, with no value. He collects them for parts.

As dinner drew to a close and everyone began pushing the tables aside to make room for what looked like it was going to be some very lively fox trotting, I knew it was time to make my exit. "I hate to eat and run," I told them, "but I really must be getting home. I've got a lot of work to do."

In Downtown, dating is even more challenging for the handful of single women who live here. Think about it. If you post a photo online, it's likely that about 99.9 percent of the men will know who you are. And even if they don't know you, there's a good chance that you'll run into them in PRICE-LESS, or at the gym or dump at some point. And horrors! Imagine when they recognize you from your photo on the online dating site. No, online dating really isn't an option here in Downtown. Unless, of course, you're willing to travel to a faraway city for a rendez-vous, and thus ensure that your blind date isn't someone you already know.

Of course, you could try the old-fashioned newspaper ads. But you're likely to only attract those old-fashioned men whose sole way of looking for a date is to scour the old-fashioned newspaper ads. I did once try that. My ad read: Seeking an available male for dinner, drinking and dancing. Must have car, job and teeth. Hard to believe, but I never received any responses. And that, my friends, is why I am still a single woman in Downtown.

Don't touch that dial

Who remembers their first transistor radio? Younger readers might ask: Transistor radio? What's that? Perhaps you can find one in your parents' – or grandparents' – basement, in that box of old stuff they can't bear to part with: a typewriter, a dial phone, a Walkman, a couple of old music tapes and maybe some record albums. Recently, I was at my friend Mary Ann's house and she brought out a small transistor radio in a black leather case, with a carrying strap. She tried to dial in a radio station, but all we heard was static. The mere sight of this historic artifact and the sounds of static brought back a flood of memories.

The Christmas when I got my first transistor radio, at age nine, I thought I had really hit the big time. This radio meant that I could actually listen to music in my own bedroom. The radio was AM only, and the local radio station WWTF was the only one on the air. Or, more accurately, it was the only station that I could tune in on with my spiffy new device. Did I mention that this station was only on the air during daylight hours? In winter, that meant that they stopped broadcasting around 4 pm. Maybe it was because there was only one person working at the station, and he wanted to get home before dark. As spring approached, and the days started getting longer, I discovered, to my delight, that WWTF was broadcasting longer hours. Maybe they had hired a second announcer to work the second shift? Or did their radio waves really only work during daylight hours? No matter. I was just happy that I could listen to my radio later into the evening.

Although I don't believe the WWTF announcer ever actually said, "Don't touch that dial!" it didn't occur to me to even try to tune in another station. After all, it was the only station I could find when I originally received my radio. And so, I resigned myself to the fact that my device simply wasn't capable of receiving signals from any place outside our town.

That is, until one evening in early summer, when I was bored and started fiddling with the dial. Imagine my surprise when I came across a station that was playing 'cool' music, the kind I actually wanted to listen to. There it was, coming in loud and clear – assuming I could manage to adjust the little line so that it was just in exactly the right place on the dial: It was a New York City radio station, with the DJ playing everything from Motown to Elvis to Bobby Darrin and Chubby Checker. There were songs about gruesome car crashes: Dead Man's Curve, Teen Angel, Last Kiss, Tell Laura I Love Her. Or about bad relationships: It's My Party, He's a Rebel, Leader of the Pack. And so much more. Overnight, my horizons had exploded, suddenly extending far beyond my town and all the way to the big city of New York. I was connected!

Admittedly, 'connected' has an entirely different meaning today, when we can talk to people in Europe, China, Africa or anywhere else via Skype or online chats, and when – thanks to the Internet – we can listen to any radio station in the world. Gone are the days of fiddling with that tiny dial to try to find something other than static. Today we can hear any genre we want by simply typing the term into our search engine.

But believe me, when I was growing up in tiny little Downtown – long before iPods, the Internet and cell phones – getting connected to that famous DJ in New York City was huge progress. It was all the connectivity I needed.

Independent living

As the saying goes, the only two things in life that are certain are death and taxes. Here's a third certainty for most: growing old. In former times, it was common for children to take care of their aging parents. But in today's world, with families scattered across the country – or even around the world – many older folks need to look at alternative living arrangements for their sunset years.

Mom decided on her own several years ago that she wanted to move into an independent living facility. She was tired of seeing dead mice in her basement – and sometimes live ones in her living room. She had skidded on the icy roads one time too many, and had begun to worry about the day when the state wouldn't let her renew her driver's license. It was time, she said, to let others take care of plumbing problems, shoveling the driveway and live-in animals. Yes, it was time to move out of Downtown.

It was a bit of a process, since it also meant convincing her that the contents of her four-bedroom house simply wouldn't fit into the one-bedroom apartment she'd be moving into. And since she couldn't bear to part with anything, the job of cleaning out her house fell to her children and grandchildren. This meant sorting through everything from our kindergarten teachers' reports to grandma and grandpa's love letters and photos from ancestors we never knew we had. When it comes to the old photographs, I say if you don't know who it is, there's no sense in keeping it. Others in the family preferred to make a game of it. So Jennifer sits in the corner reading aloud passages from 19th century love letters while Ed labels the photos with random names from those letters. Who will ever know if that's really our distant uncle Reginald who fought in the Civil War or great-great grandma Ella Bell? Meanwhile, Lisa sorts through a box of papers that contains, among other things, grandpa's school report cards and letters from headmasters commenting on his raucous behavior.

Once we've sorted through everything, we call in an appraiser to tell us what, if anything is valuable. Of course, just because it won't bring money on the antiques market doesn't mean it has no value. For instance, there's that plate I had cookies on after school.

It was likely purchased for a few dollars 50 years ago and might be worth 50 cents at a yard sale today. But I wouldn't sell it for anything. As we move through the house picking out what we want to keep, we aren't choosing things that the appraiser considers valuable. I want that cookie plate; Lisa has her heart set on the children's tea set that she used for tea parties. Ed wants the knife opener he made in seventh grade woodworking class.

Mom settled in quickly to her new digs. She made a lot of friends and got involved in almost all the activities that were offered. In no time, she had become the champion ski jumper on the Wii machine. She really gets into tricking out her walker, based on her mood and the season. She adorns it with green tinsel and shamrocks for St. Patrick's Day. During the Christmas season, she puts sleigh bells on it and reindeer horns. Outside the dining room, all the walkers are lined up at dinnertime – which means about 4:30 pm, but mom's always stands out!

One of the regular activities is a movie after dinner. Mom told us that she was looking forward to the next movie because the plan was to follow up the movie with a discussion. When I called the next day to ask how it went, Mom said that most of the residents were asleep by the end of the movie, so they decided to do the discussion the next evening. The problem, Mom said, was that, by the next evening, most residents had trouble remembering the name of the movie, let alone anything about the plot and characters. I know that feeling!

A life well-lived

After many years of living in a senior living facility, Mom passed away. She was 97, and death at that age isn't exactly unexpected. But then again, when the end does finally come, it's still a jarring shock for those left behind. So final. But at least she died the way we would all like to go – quickly and painlessly, according to the doctor.

She said years ago that she was ready to go whenever her time came. She wasn't depressed about it, just realistic. In fact, she made many preparations during the final decades of her life. When Dad died in 1982, she ordered a gravestone carved with both his and her names and birthdates plus his date of death. You can just add my date of death later, she told me. It's cheaper and easier that way. She also wrote her own obituary years ago. I wondered if she didn't trust us to get it right or if she was just trying to make things easy for us. As for the photo to go with it, she wanted one where she looked good, but not too good. After all, she said, people should know that she had lived to be as old as she was. She hated reading the obituary of a woman who was 90-something, juxtaposed with a photo of a glamorous young girl. We were not to do that for her, she instructed.

As Mom grew older, her aches and pains became debilitating and her eyesight failed. She needed help to get dressed, to go to the bathroom and even to eat. This downward spiral was hard on her, a woman who had always been fiercely independent. But perhaps the most difficult for her was when she started, over the last year, to lose her mental sharpness. Some days were worse than others. At first it was rather comical, and she laughed with us about it. She saw boxes and books everywhere in her apartment and couldn't stand the mess. We told her that they weren't really there, that she only imagined them, and that her apartment was actually neat as a pin. She said she knew all that, but she still saw the books and boxes. We joked with her that, back in the 60s, we paid good money for drugs to get us to the state she was in.

In the last months, she became obsessed with time. While helping her organize the imaginary boxes and books one day, my brother and I found five minute-minders, along with countless watches and clocks, in drawers and on shelves. "What do you need all these for, Mom?" we asked. "Well, I just want to be sure I have plenty of time," she replied with a wry smile. We also found enough rubber bands and paper clips to stock an office supply store. Perhaps she needed those to hold things together as it all started to fall apart.

She also told us that she wanted to move up to the third floor of her facility to be with my dad – who had passed away many years ago. The building had no third floor, but she kept searching for the stairs to get up there. We told her that she would find them when her room was ready up there.

Our joking was never insensitive. She laughed with us, finding humor in little things, even when life got really tough. "Teach your children well" as the song goes. And that's just what she did, showing us how to live life to the fullest. Here's to Mom. To a life well-lived, to her new life on the third floor and to the memories that will always live on.

Southern comfort zone

One winter, I decided to try spending time somewhere other than Downtown. I packed my car and headed south. I didn't actually consider it to be a scary thing to do, even though friends and family members kept telling me how brave they thought I was. Brave? Heck, I've parachuted out of an airplane, given birth in a VW bus, gotten arrested in East Germany and spent winters in Downtown. Striking out on my own for parts unknown was not something that could scare me.

No, I viewed this as just another adventure. Something to push me out of my comfort zone. Many friends offered advice – most of which wasn't all that useful. But perhaps the strangest advice of all came from a woman I had recently met, who told me she had a lot of travel experience. I don't actually think she had been on many road trips, but she did seem to have a lot of road behind her. Her words of wisdom for me? Keep your guns close and don't hang any clothes in your car window.

I briefly considered joining ancestry.com ahead of time so that I could find some long-lost sixth cousins along my route – who didn't know I exist – and invite myself to spend the night with them. Why pay for hotels and dinner when I could grace relatives with my magnetic presence? And I definitely know how to be the perfect houseguest, as you can learn in another chapter of this book. But, in the end, I decided this might be asking too much of people that I don't even know. And besides, what would I say if they wanted to come visit me in Downtown next summer and stay for much longer than one night!

During my drive south I encountered a number of characters. There was the guy in the convenience store in southern Virginia who, out of the blue, while standing next to me at the coffee machine, launched into a rant about all the people on welfare and how much tax he is paying. I didn't know why he picked me to unload upon and I also had no idea about how to respond. So – unbelievable as it may sound for those who know me – I held my tongue. Despite his rant, and his apparent disdain for northerners – I guess he had noticed my northern license plate – he did call me 'ma'am' several times during his raging discourse. Wow, a polite ranter!

As I ventured ever deeper into the south, I became ever more impressed with the people I was meeting. I attribute this to the fact that everyone was calling me 'ma'am.' I liked that. I can't recall anyone in Downtown ever using that term with me. Or with anyone else, for that matter. The waitress in the breakfast room at the Quality Inn near Savannah not only called me 'ma'am', she also called me sugar (or more accurately, shoogah). And honey. I was definitely feeling the southern hospitality.

Upon arriving in Florida, it didn't take me long to find the perfect town to settle into as my new winter home. With its miles of sandy Gulf Coast beaches, restaurants, grocery stores and gas stations on nearly every corner, a library, a theater, and music everywhere, what's not to like? And yet, because this place is slightly off the beaten path, it doesn't have the crowds that plague many other resort towns. No traffic jams, laid back, friendly people enjoying life in the slow lane – a lot like Downtown. Just without the snow! But here's another similarity to Downtown: When I mention to locals how much I love this town, they beg me not to tell anyone about it because they don't want any more people moving here. My slogan for Downtown, and for this 'secret' town, is "Hard to get there, harder to leave." But of course my heart is still in Downtown. So, come spring, I loaded my bags in my car and headed back 'home.' After all, I knew they needed me back there to supervise the rolling out of the sidewalks.

Acknowledgements

This book could not have been written without the support and encouragement of countless friends and family members. A special shout-out to Judy, Seddon and Peggy, for their valuable feedback and eagle-eye proofreading. Thanks to Lina for showing me the ropes of self-publishing. And to Mary Ann, for her input and never-ending inspiration to keep on writing. I feel very lucky to have had Mary's superb artistic talents in helping to design the cover of the book. Special thanks to Sally, preserver and purveyor of historical facts and fiction. Thank you, too, to everyone who has ever listened to or read my stories, to all who believed that this book would actually get written, even if it was later rather than sooner. And many thanks to all my friends, family and readers in Germany, too. Many of the stories in this book are based on columns I have written for a German magazine that describe 'life in America.' Of course, we should not take any of these tales too seriously – though it can rightfully be said that truth is often stranger than fiction.